Dear Parent:

Congratulations! Your child is taking the first steps on an exciting journey. The destination? Independent reading!

STEP INTO READING® will help your child get there. The program offers five steps to reading success. Each step includes fun stories and colorful art. There are also Step into Reading Sticker Books, Step into Reading Math Readers, Step into Reading Write-In Readers, Step into Reading Phonics Readers, and Step into Reading Phonics First Steps! Boxed Sets—a complete literacy program with something for every child.

Learning to Read, Step by Step!

Ready to Read   Preschool–Kindergarten
• big type and easy words • rhyme and rhythm • picture clues
For children who know the alphabet and are eager to begin reading.

Reading with Help   Preschool–Grade 1
• basic vocabulary • short sentences • simple stories
For children who recognize familiar words and sound out new words with help.

Reading on Your Own   Grades 1–3
• engaging characters • easy-to-follow plots • popular topics
For children who are ready to read on their own.

Reading Paragraphs   Grades 2–3
• challenging vocabulary • short paragraphs • exciting stories
For newly independent readers who read simple sentences with confidence.

Ready for Chapters   Grades 2–4
• chapters • longer paragraphs • full-color art
For children who want to take the plunge into chapter books but still like colorful pictures.

STEP INTO READING® is designed to give every child a successful reading experience. The grade levels are only guides. Children can progress through the steps at their own speed, developing confidence in their reading, no matter what their grade.

Remember, a lifetime love of reading starts with a single step!

www.stepintoreading.com
www.randomhouse.com/kids/disney

Educators and librarians, for a variety of teaching tools, visit us at
www.randomhouse.com/teachers

Library of Congress Cataloging-in-Publication Data
Tyler, Amy J.
Best dad in the sea / by Amy J. Tyler.   p. cm. — (Step into reading. A step 1 book)
At head of title: Disney-Pixar.
"Finding Nemo."
SUMMARY: When Nemo gets caught on his way to school, his father comes to the rescue.
ISBN-13: 978-0-7364-2131-7 (trade) — ISBN-13: 978-0-7364-8021-5 (lib. bdg.)
ISBN-10: 0-7364-2131-9 (trade) — ISBN-10: 0-7364-8021-8 (lib. bdg.)
[1. Fishes—Fiction. 2. Fathers and sons—Fiction.]
I. Finding Nemo (Motion Picture). II. Title. III. Series: Step into Reading. Step 1 book.

PZ7.T9367 Be 2003 [E]—dc21 2002014819

MANUFACTURED IN CHINA   40 39 38 37

STEP INTO READING, RANDOM HOUSE, and the Random House colophon are registered trademarks
and the Step into Reading colophon is a trademark of Random House, Inc.

Disney · PIXAR
FINDING NEMO

BEST DAD IN THE SEA

By Amy J. Tyler

Illustrated by the Disney Storybook Artists

Designed by Disney's Global Design Group

Random House New York

Nemo loves his dad,
Marlin.
And Marlin loves Nemo.

But they are
very different.

Marlin is careful.

"Slow down, Nemo!"

Nemo is not.

"Come on, Dad!"

One day, Nemo is
TOO brave.

He swims far ahead.

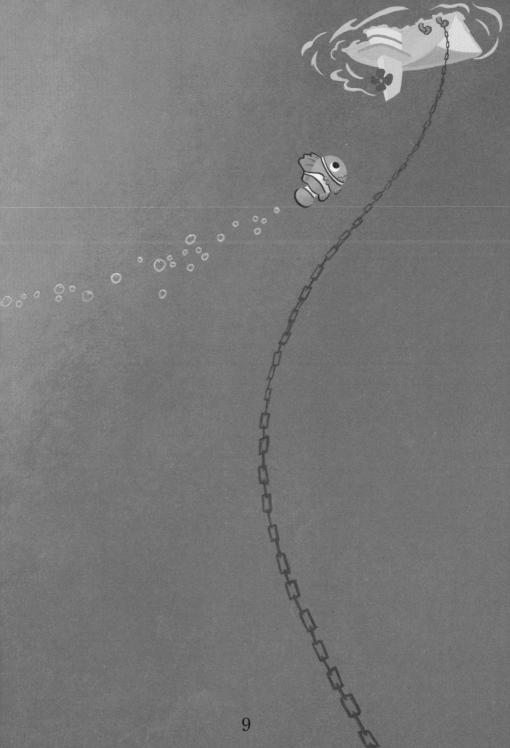

Oh, no! A diver.
Marlin cannot
see Nemo.

Nemo has been caught!

Marlin swims
after Nemo.
But he is too late.

PLOP!

Into a tank Nemo goes.

How will he
ever get home?

Marlin is sad.

He wants to search
for Nemo.

His friend Dory can help.

At first,
Marlin is very,
very afraid.

But not for long.

"My son needs me!"

Marlin says.

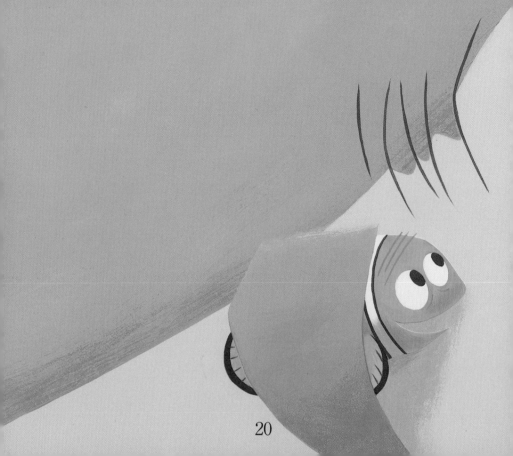

For Nemo,
Marlin is brave.

He is VERY brave!

Nemo hears
good news.

Help is on the way.

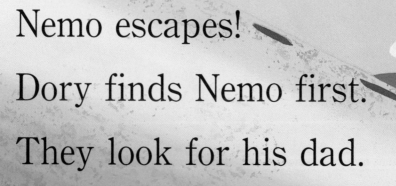

Nemo escapes!

Dory finds Nemo first.

They look for his dad.

They ask the crabs
for help.

They find Marlin.
But they get stuck
in a net.

Nemo has a plan.
"Swim down!" he says
to the fish.

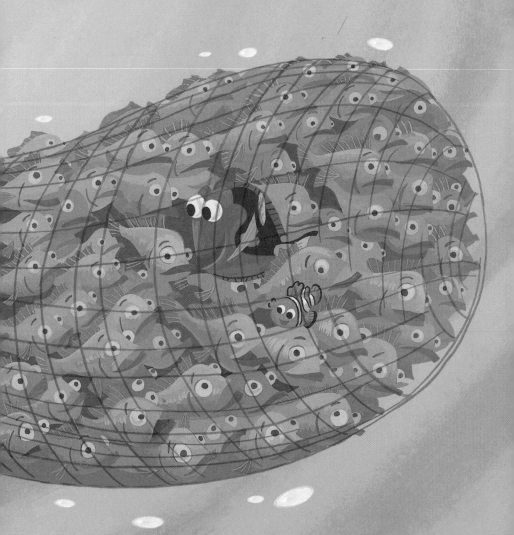

They are free!

"You were so brave,"

says Nemo.

"You were brave, too,"

says his dad.

Nemo loves his dad.
And his dad loves him.

And they are not
so different after all!